I Wish I was an Alien

7

Published by
Evans Brothers Limited
2A Portman Mansions
Chiltern St
London W1U 6NR

Reprinted 2010

British Library Cataloguing in Publication Data

French, Vivian
        I wish I was an alien. - (Zig zags)
        1. Children's stories - Pictorial works
        I. Title
        823.9'14 [J]

ISBN: 978 0 237 52776 1

Printed in Spain by Graficas94

Series Editor: Nick Turpin
Design: Robert Walster
Production: Jenny Mulvanny
Series Consultant: Gill Matthews

ZIG ZAG

I Wish I Was an Alien

by Vivian French

illustrated by Lisa Williams

Evans

I wish I was an alien floating up in space.

5

I wouldn't have to clean my teeth.

I'd go and check out Jupiter.

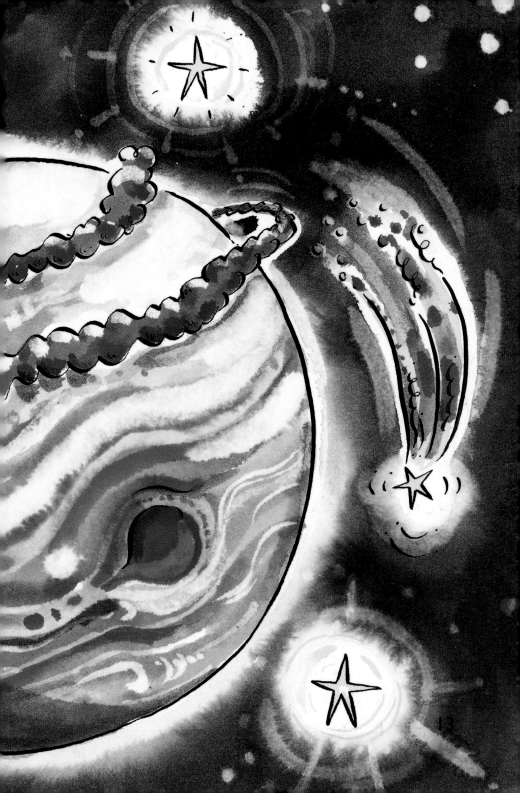

I wish I was a boy on Earth
and didn't live in space.
I wouldn't have these
tentacles, instead I'd
have a face.

19

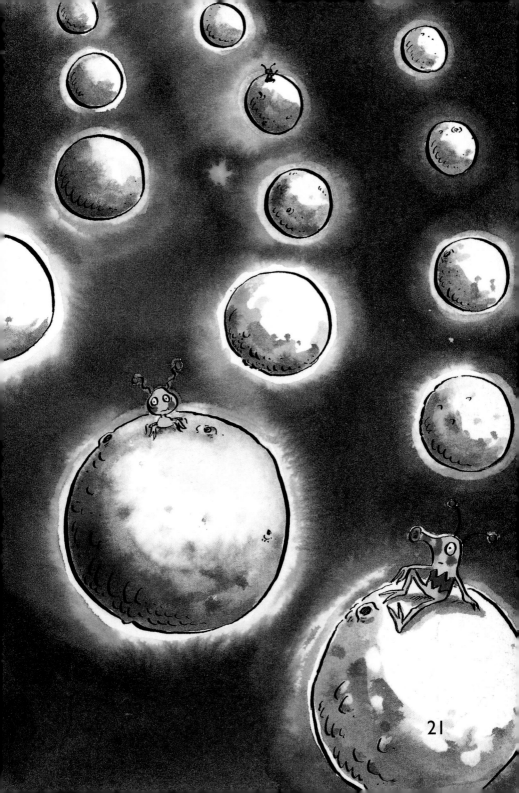

I want to ride on buses...

23

...and I want to go to school.

29

30

Why not try reading another ZigZag book?

Dinosaur Planet　　　　　　　　　　ISBN 9780237527938
by David Orme and Fabiano Fiorin

Tall Tilly　　　　　　　　　　　　　ISBN 9780237527945
by Jillian Powell and Tim Archbold

Batty Betty's Spells　　　　　　　　ISBN 9780237527952
by Hilary Robinson and Belinda Worsley

The Thirsty Moose　　　　　　　　ISBN 9780237527921
by David Orme and Mike Gordon

The Clumsy Cow　　　　　　　　　ISBN 9780237527907
by Julia Moffat and Lisa Williams

Open Wide!　　　　　　　　　　　ISBN 9780237527914
by Julia Moffatt and Anni Axworthy

Too Small　　　　　　　　　　　　ISBN 9780237527778
by Kay Woodward and Deborah van de Leigraaf

I Wish I Was An Alien　　　　　　　ISBN 9780237527761
by Vivian French and Lisa Williams

The Disappearing Cheese　　　　　ISBN 9780237527754
by Paul Harrison and Ruth Rivers

Terry the Flying Turtle　　　　　　ISBN 9780237527747
by Anna Wilson and Mike Gordon

Pet To School Day　　　　　　　　ISBN 9780237527730
by Hilary Robinson and Tim Archbold

The Cat in the Coat　　　　　　　ISBN 9780237527723
by Vivian French and Alison Bartlett

Pig in Love　　　　　　　　　　　ISBN 9780237529505
by Vivian French and Tim Archbold

The Donkey That Was Too Fast　　ISBN 9780237529499
by David Orme and Ruth Rivers

The Yellow Balloon　　　　　　　ISBN 9780237529482
by Helen Bird and Simona Dimitri

Hamish Finds Himself　　　　　　ISBN 9780237529475
by Jillian Powell and Belinda Worsley

Flying South　　　　　　　　　　ISBN 9780237529468
by Alan Durant and Kath Lucas

Croc by the Rock　　　　　　　　ISBN 9780237529451
by Hilary Robinson and Mike Gordon

Turn off the Telly!　　　　　　　ISBN 9780237531683
by Charlie Gardner and Barbara Nascimbeni

Fred and Finn　　　　　　　　　ISBN 9780237531690
by Madeline Goodey and Mike Gordon

A Mouse in the House　　　　　　ISBN 9780237531676
by Vivian French and Tim Archbold

Lovely, Lovely Pirate Gold　　　　ISBN 9780237531706
by Scoular Anderson